THOMAS & FRIENDS

No More Mr. Nice Engine!

A Random House PICTUREBACK® Book

Random House New York

Thomas the Tank Engine & Friends™

CREATED BY BRITT ALLCROFT

Based on The Railway Series by The Reverend W Awdry.
Copyright © 2014 Gullane (Thomas) LLC.
Thomas the Tank Engine & Friends and Thomas & Friends are trademarks of Gullane (Thomas) Limited. HIT and the HIT Entertainment logo are trademarks of HIT Entertainment Limited. All rights reserved. Published in the United States by Random House Children's Books, a division of Random House, Inc., 1745 Broadway, New York, NY 10019, and in Canada by Random House of Canada Limited, Toronto. Pictureback, Random House, and the Random House colophon are registered trademarks of Random House, Inc.

randomhouse.com/kids   www.thomasandfriends.com

ISBN 978-0-385-37508-5

MANUFACTURED IN CHINA 10 9 8 7 6 5 4 3 2

Hiro was one of the strongest engines on the Island of Sodor. He was also polite and kind.

"After you, Thomas," Hiro said when the engines arrived at the Washdown at the same time.

One morning, Diesel was shunting some Troublesome Trucks that Edward had brought from the dairy. Diesel gave the trucks a bump to make them get in line.

"Stop biffing the trucks, Diesel. You're spilling the milk!" Edward cried.

"Mind your own business," Diesel said rudely.

When Hiro arrived to pull the trucks, he greeted everyone with a smile.

"Oh, Hiro! Don't be such a Mr. Nice Engine! These trucks are nothing but troublesome. You need to show them who's boss!" Diesel said.

Hiro told Diesel the trucks would be no trouble. "I am Master of the Railway," he said.

Hiro collected the trucks and puffed away.

Soon the trucks started biffing and bashing each other.

Hiro chuckled. "You can try to be troublesome, but I am Master of the Railway. You won't be any trouble for me!"

He didn't know that Diesel had spilled the milk.

The trucks made Hiro bump and judder, but he puffed on to Knapford Station.

When Sir Topham Hatt opened the door to the milk truck, out poured the spilled milk! "Oh, no! My trousers!" he exclaimed.

Hiro was shocked. "I'm so sorry, Sir!" he peeped.

"I hope you'll be more careful on your next job!" Sir Topham said as he left to get his trousers cleaned.

Hiro felt very bad.

"What's the matter with you?" Diesel asked when he saw Hiro at Brendam Docks.

Hiro told him how the milk had spilled on Sir Topham's trousers. "I feel so ashamed," he said.

Diesel was relieved not to be blamed. "I told you the trucks were trouble! You should have shown them who's boss—given them a biff!"

"No," Hiro replied. "It's always best to be polite and kind." He puffed away with some other trucks, including one with a load of heavy cream. He didn't know that Diesel followed him to make mischief.

The Troublesome Trucks biffed and bashed, but Hiro was still polite and gentle.

At a red signal, Diesel coupled up to the trucks.

When Hiro puffed up a hill, Diesel put on his brakes to slow the trucks down. Hiro made it to the top, but when they went down the other side, Diesel helped the trucks go very fast.

Thomas saw them whoosh past. "Wow! What's going on?" he peeped.

When Diesel biffed the trucks from behind, they laughed.

"That's it!" Hiro said at last. "No more Mr. Nice Engine! I am Master of the Railway! I'll show you!"

As he entered Knapford Station, he braked so suddenly that the trucks crunched together.

Big barrels flew into the air and smashed on the ground, splattering everyone with cream!

"My trousers!" cried Sir Topham.

Diesel tried to sneak away, but Thomas pulled up, blocking him.

"Why was Diesel pushing you and the Troublesome Trucks?" Thomas asked Hiro.

"Were you the one biffing and bashing me?" Hiro asked Diesel.

"And he spilled your milk this morning," Edward added.

Sir Topham was very disappointed with Diesel. "You will learn from Hiro how to look after Troublesome Trucks properly!" he said.

So Hiro worked with Diesel. "Remember, be polite and kind!" Hiro said when Diesel tried to jostle the trucks.

"Oops! Sorry, Hiro," Diesel said. "Nice trucks. Good trucks."

The Troublesome Trucks giggled. Hiro looked proud and happy.

Sir Topham Hatt was pleased that James had delivered the fish on time. "You are a Really Useful Engine," he said. "But you are also a Really Smelly Engine!" He told James to go to the Washdown.

"Yes, Sir," peeped James. He even smiled.

"I had a little accident with some fish crates," James explained.
And there was still a fish stuck on his chassis!

"What's that smell?" Emily asked when James returned to the sheds.
"That's the smell of James," Thomas said, laughing.

The fishy smell grew even stronger as James rushed around the countryside making deliveries. He couldn't wait to get clean again.

Baldwin rolled up. "You're supposed to take the fish *in* the trucks, not carry them by yourself!" he said, smiling. Now James was grumpier than ever.

The fish Cranky was unloading spilled in a heap on James.

"James is scared of the smelly fish!" the trucks repeated.
As James got ready to bash them again, he backed into Cranky's hook.

The trucks laughed. "James is scared of the smelly fish!"
"I am not," James huffed. He bashed the trucks to make them behave.

When James arrived at the docks, Cranky was loading the Troublesome Trucks with fish.

James didn't want to get any fish on himself.

James explained that he'd changed his mind about delivering the fish because they were so smelly.

"But you told Henry you would take that train," Sir Topham said.

Sir Topham told James that he would have to pull the *Flying Kipper* that night to make up for his broken promise.

"And I expect the fish to be delivered on time!"

"That wasn't a dream, Henry!" peeped Thomas. "I heard James say that."

The other engines agreed that they'd heard the same thing.

Sir Topham turned to James. "Is this true? Are you the one who caused confusion and delay?"

Henry was late with every delivery. Back at the sheds, Sir Topham Hatt asked him what had happened.

"Sorry, Sir," Henry replied. "I must have overslept. I dreamed that James said he'd pull the *Flying Kipper* for me."

James made his way to Brendam Docks to collect the *Flying Kipper* and its load of fresh fish. But as he got closer, he noticed a funny smell. He quickly changed his mind and returned to the sheds to wake Henry.

"But I thought *you* were delivering the fish tonight," said Henry.

"You must have been dreaming," James said slyly.

Henry hurried to the docks to get the *Flying Kipper*.

"Percy doesn't like your stories, James!" Thomas peeped.

"It's not my fault Percy's not as brave as I am," James replied.

Henry spoke up. "If you're really not afraid, then prove it by pulling the *Flying Kipper* for me tonight!"

"Okay, Henry, I shall!" James huffed.

"Better you than me, delivering all that fish," Thomas said with a laugh.

One night, James was telling scary stories in Tidmouth Sheds.

"The ghost train rattled over the bridge, waking everyone with its spooky whistle. *Whooooooo . . .*"

Percy thought the stories were very scary. He often pulled the Mail Train at night, when things sometimes look scarier than they really are.

A Random House PICTUREBACK® Book

Random House New York

Thomas the Tank Engine & Friends™

CREATED BY BRITT ALLCROFT

Based on The Railway Series by The Reverend W Awdry.
Copyright © 2014 Gullane (Thomas) LLC.
Thomas the Tank Engine & Friends and Thomas & Friends are trademarks of Gullane (Thomas) Limited. HIT and the HIT Entertainment logo are trademarks of HIT Entertainment Limited. All rights reserved. Published in the United States by Random House Children's Books, a division of Random House, Inc., 1745 Broadway, New York, NY 10019, and in Canada by Random House of Canada Limited, Toronto. Pictureback, Random House, and the Random House colophon are registered trademarks of Random House, Inc.

randomhouse.com/kids   www.thomasandfriends.com

ISBN 978-0-385-37508-5

MANUFACTURED IN CHINA 10 9 8 7 6 5 4 3 2

HiT entertainment